STEP-BY-STEP

MAKING JEWELRY

SARA GRISEWOOD

ILLUSTRATED BY JIM ROBINS

Kingfisher

NEW YORK

KINGFISHER
Larousse Kingfisher Chambers Inc.
95 Madison Avenue
New York, New York 10016

First American edition 1995

10 9 8 7 6 5 4 3 2 1 (RLB)
10 9 8 7 6 5 4 3 2 1 (PB)

Copyright © Larousse plc 1995

All rights reserved under
International and Pan-American
Copyright Conventions.

LIBRARY OF CONGRESS
CATALOGING-IN-PUBLICATION DATA
Grisewood, Sara.
Making jewelry/Sara Grisewood.
p.   cm.—(Step-by-step)
1. Jewelry making—Juvenile
literature.   [1. Jewelry making.
2. Handicraft.] I. Title. II. Series:
Step-by-step (Kingfisher Books)
TT212.G75   1995
745.594´2—dc20
94-44862 CIP AC

ISBN 1-85697-589-4 (RLB)
ISBN 1-85697-588-6 (PB)

Series editor: Deri Robins
Editor: Clare Oliver
Series designer: Ben White
Illustrator: Jim Robins
Photographer: Steve Shott
Cover designer: Terry Woodley

Printed in Hong Kong

CONTENTS

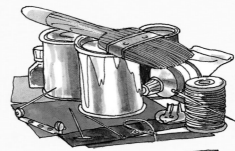

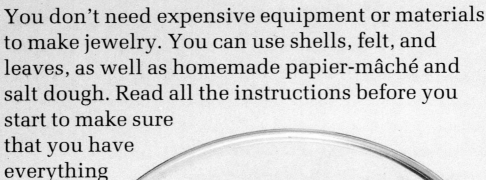

WHAT YOU NEED

You don't need expensive equipment or materials to make jewelry. You can use shells, felt, and leaves, as well as homemade papier-mâché and salt dough. Read all the instructions before you start to make sure that you have everything you need.

Paint

Varnis

Flour

Wallpaper paste

Rolling pin

Colored clay

Salt

Special Things

Findings are the special fastenings used to make jewelry. Necklaces can be tied with a knot, but you'll need findings for pins and earrings.

Craft stores sell findings, as well as beads, sequins, and fake gemstones.

Paper clips are ideal for pendant hooks—just stick them into the jewelry before baking. For threading heavy beads, buy a strong thread, such as linen carpet thread.

Tools of the Trade

You'll need scissors, a craft knife, glue (a safe but strong epoxy glue), a pencil, metal ruler, masking tape, sewing thread, and needles.

An ordinary knife, fork and spoon, and a rolling pin make ideal tools for modeling. Work on an old board. Bake beads on metal skewers.

Buy colored clay, such as Fimo. Keep paper and wallpaper paste on hand for papier-mâché, and flour, salt, and water for salt dough (see page 6). You'll also need paints, brushes, and varnish (see pages 8–9).

String

Needle

Felt

Shells

Strong thread

Brush

Newspaper

Craft knife

Modeling tools

Findings

Scissors

Epoxy glue

Bought beads

Leaves

Colored clay is ideal for making jewelry and doesn't even need a coat of paint. Other modeling materials, such as salt dough and papier-mâché, can be made at home very cheaply.

Making Salt Dough

Stir together $\frac{1}{2}$ cup of salt with 3 cups of sifted flour. Slowly add between $7\frac{1}{2}$ and 12 fl. ounces of warm water.

Mix together to make a soft dough. Knead until smooth, then leave it in a plastic bag for half an hour before using.

Bake your pieces at 340°F. Beads and pins take between $\frac{1}{2}$–$1\frac{1}{2}$ hours. Ask an adult to tap them—if they sound hollow, they are ready.

Making Papier-Mâché

Old cereal boxes will make ideal cardboard bases for your jewelry. Cover your base with layers of torn newspaper dipped in wallpaper paste. The smaller the strips, the smoother your jewelry will be. Let the papier-mâché dry between layers.

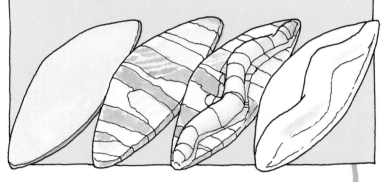

Using Colored Clay

You can buy colored clay from craft and toy stores—it even comes in metallic and fluorescent colors! Always follow the instructions on the package before baking. Work on a board and clean your work surface before you change colors.

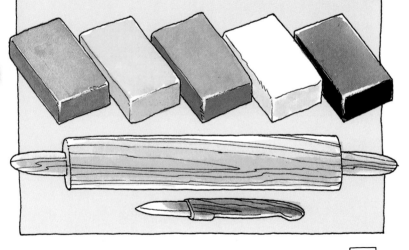

Finish off salt-dough and papier-mâché pieces by painting and varnishing them. Varnish also stops decorations from falling off and protects fragile objects, such as leaves—after all, painting isn't the only way to decorate your jewelry.

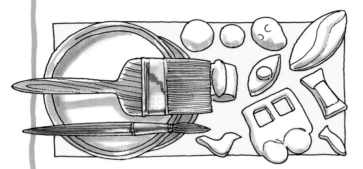

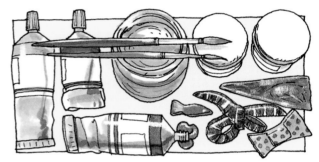

Paints and Brushes

Always let salt-dough jewelry cool and papier-mâché objects dry before painting. Apply a coat of white latex paint first so that you have a smooth, white surface to decorate. It will keep newsprint from showing through on your papier-mâché pieces.

Acrylic paints are best if you want really dazzling results, but poster paints give bright colors, too, and are much cheaper. Latex, acrylics, and poster paints are all water-based, so all you'll need to clean your brushes is plenty of water.

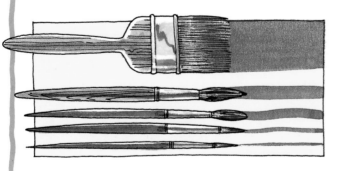

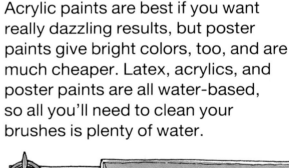

Keep a selection of brushes handy. A large, thick brush is best for the base coat, but you'll need finer ones for painting details, especially on homemade beads.

When you have lots of beads to paint, thread them on metal skewers. Rest the needle across an open shoe box, then paint. Leave the beads on the needle until they are all dry.

Using a cloth to rub gold paint on top of green will make your jewelry look like a valuable antique!

Tricks with Paint

After the latex paint, apply a base color. When this is dry, use a fine brush to paint a pattern on top.

Try smearing paint onto wood with your fingers. This gives an uneven and unusual stained effect.

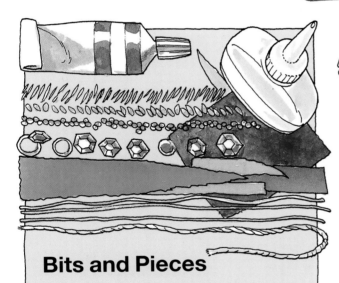

Bits and Pieces

You can glue all sorts of daring decorations onto your jewelry. Use a strong epoxy glue or ordinary white glue.

Gems, natural objects (such as seeds), and even string can all be used as unusual surface decorations. The only limit is your imagination!

Varnishing

Give all your painted jewelry a glossy coat of polyurethane varnish. It makes the paint really shine and stops it from chipping.

When varnishing, make sure there is enough air in the room. Varnish can be dangerous if you breathe in too much of it. Always keep the window wide open.

9

BRILLIANT PINS

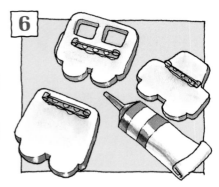

These pins will really brighten up a jacket or coat! We used colored clay for the balloon and the musical pins and added layers of clay to make raised patterns—this is called "relief" decoration.

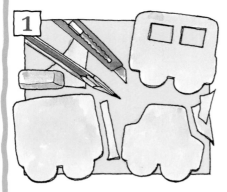

Salt-dough Pins

1 Draw and cut out simple shapes on cardboard to use as templates for your pins.

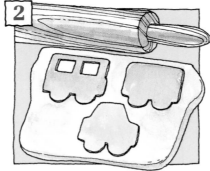

2 Roll out a slab of salt dough to about $\frac{1}{3}$ inch thick. Put the templates on the dough.

3 Now cut around the templates. You can cut out holes for windows too, if you want.

4 To mark the edges of the windows or wheels, dig into the dough with a fingernail or knife.

5 Bake the pins in the oven. Leave them to cool, then paint and varnish the fronts.

6 Stick a finding to the back, using a strong glue. Let the glue dry, then wear your pin!

To make this hot-air balloon, you'll need to roll very thin layers of colored clay. Try not to smudge them!

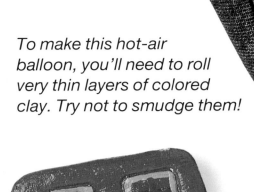

Salt dough is just the thing for these chunky, colorful pins.

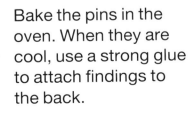

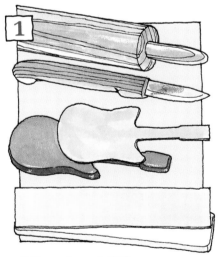

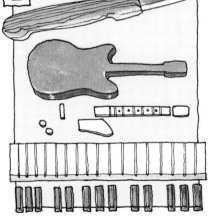

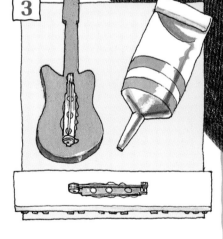

Musical Pins

1 Make templates for the guitar and keyboard. Place them on $\frac{1}{4}$-inch-thick colored clay and cut around them.

2 Cut out piano keys and the guitar trimmings and press into place. Mark piano keys and guitar frets with a knife.

3 Bake the pins in the oven. When they are cool, use a strong glue to attach findings to the back.

FLOWERS AND BOWS

Salt-dough flowers and bows make pretty pins. Bake all your pieces together, leave to cool, and then paint and varnish. Finally, glue findings to the backs. Brooches make wonderful presents—if you can bear to give these away!

Bows

Roll out some salt dough to $\frac{1}{4}$ inch thick. Then use a knife to cut a strip ($\frac{1}{2}$ in. x 6 in.), like a salt-dough ribbon.

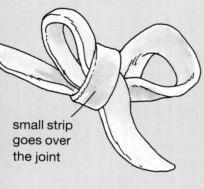

small strip goes over the joint

Loop the strip into a bow, as if it were a ribbon. Join together wherever one layer overlaps another—just dab with water and press gently. Use an extra scrap to cover the center.

To make a bow-tie pin, cut out a basic bow-tie shape and a small rectangle (for the "knot") from salt dough. Stick the knot on with a dab of water.

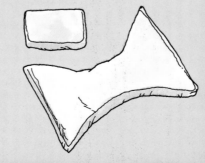

Flowers

Make a cardboard template for the petals. Cut out about ten petals from salt dough.

Overlap the petals to make a circle. Dab with water and smooth the joints.

Press a blob of dough in the center of each flower to hide where the petals joined.

For another kind of flower, cut the base with a cookie cutter. Stick four diamond-shaped petals on top.

You can also make flowers by sticking four smaller petals on top of four larger ones.

RINGS AND THINGS

Papier-mâché is perfect for making fun, chunky jewelry. You can decorate rings with jewels made from scrunched-up tissue paper. Finally, use bright paints in different colors. Let each coat of paint dry before using a new color. Always make sure your bangles and rings are big enough to slide on and off your wrist and fingers easily.

1

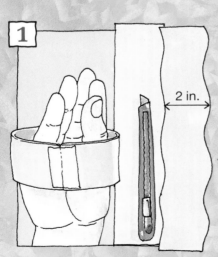

Cut two strips of thin cardboard. Give one a wavy edge. Ask a friend to hold each strip around your hand and tape it together for you.

2

Cut narrower strips to make rings. Wrap them around your finger, so they slide off easily, then tape the ends together as before.

3

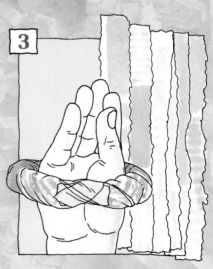

For a chunky bracelet, take six strips of newspaper and twist them together. Wrap this rope around your wrist and tape as before.

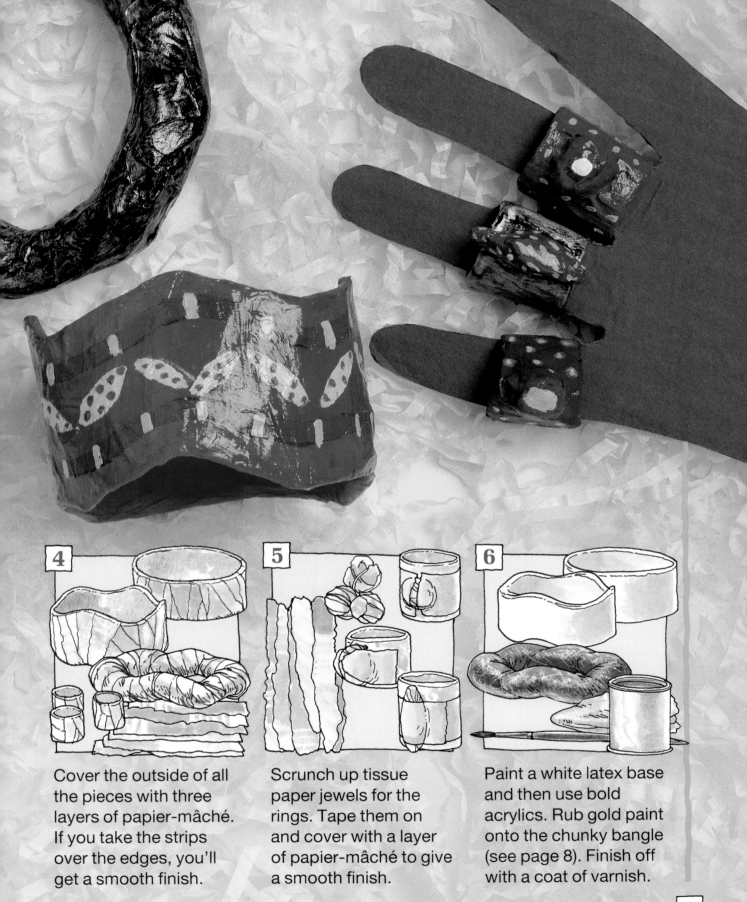

4 Cover the outside of all the pieces with three layers of papier-mâché. If you take the strips over the edges, you'll get a smooth finish.

5 Scrunch up tissue paper jewels for the rings. Tape them on and cover with a layer of papier-mâché to give a smooth finish.

6 Paint a white latex base and then use bold acrylics. Rub gold paint onto the chunky bangle (see page 8). Finish off with a coat of varnish.

BEAD NECKLACES

Salt-dough beads look great threaded together
with beads bought from craft stores.
Try making round beads, then go for new shapes,
such as the Egyptian eyes. Mix different types together—
string big, homemade beads with tiny colored glass ones.

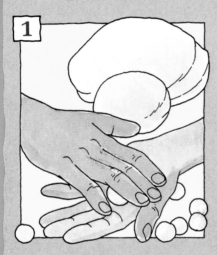

1

Pinch off a small piece
of salt dough and roll it
into a ball in your palm.

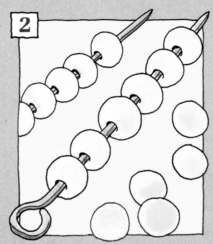

2

Push each bead onto a
metal skewer. Smooth
each bead's surface.

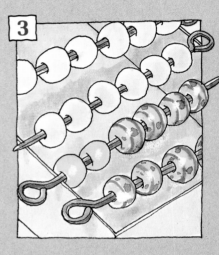

3

Bake the beads on their
skewers. Paint and
varnish when cool.

Threading Beads

Take a length of strong thread. Tape
down one end with masking tape (so
your beads don't fall off), then thread
on the beads with a needle. Peel off
the tape and knot the ends of thread
together. Feed the leftover thread
neatly back through the beads.

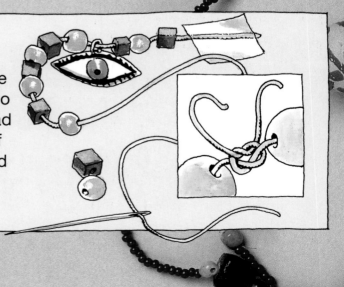

Beads don't have to be round—these are shaped like Egyptian eyes! Push in a metal paper clip before baking and thread them by the hooks.

For a lucky charm, tie red ribbon to a spare Egyptian eye bead. Pin the ribbon on with a safety pin.

BEACHCOMBING

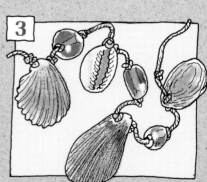

The beach is a treasure trove for jewelers! But shells can be tricky to drill, so it is usually easier to buy them with ready-drilled holes from a craft store. Show off the shells by trying out these different ways of threading.

Drilling

If you do want to use shells that you've collected yourself, ask an adult to drill holes in them for you. They will need to use a drill with a fine bit. Always wash the shells first.

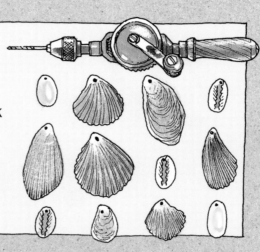

1 **2** **3**

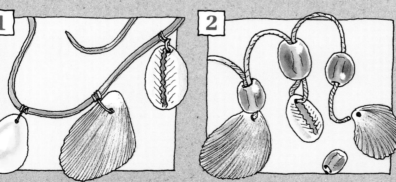

Threading Shells

With some thread, tie about three shells to the middle of a leather thong. Try using a colored thong.

Thread a bead, then a shell, then go back through the bead. Leave a space before threading the next two.

Knot some string, thread on a shell, then knot again. Leave a space, then repeat with a bead.

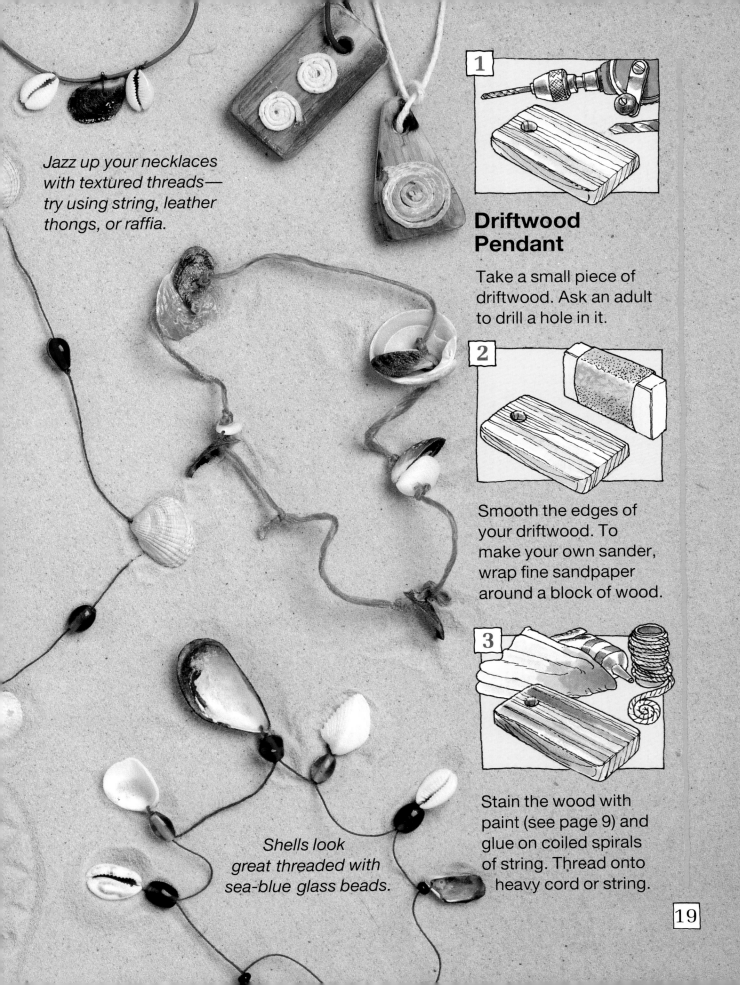

Jazz up your necklaces with textured threads— try using string, leather thongs, or raffia.

Driftwood Pendant

1

Take a small piece of driftwood. Ask an adult to drill a hole in it.

2

Smooth the edges of your driftwood. To make your own sander, wrap fine sandpaper around a block of wood.

3

Stain the wood with paint (see page 9) and glue on coiled spirals of string. Thread onto heavy cord or string.

Shells look great threaded with sea-blue glass beads.

19

EARRINGS

You can wear earrings whether your ears are pierced or not. Craft stores sell clip-on earring findings as well as ones for pierced ears. Glue clip-ons to the back of the finished earring.

Pierced Ears

Findings for pierced ears have two parts. The hook is the part that goes through your ear. It slips onto the pin. There are two different kinds of pin—head pins and eye pins.

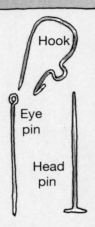

Hook

Eye pin

Head pin

Head pins are used for bead earrings. The head stops the beads from falling off (see page 25). When the beads are in place, bend around the top of the pin with tweezers to make an eye for the hook.

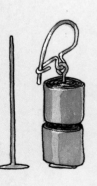

Eye pins are used for papier-mâché or salt-dough earrings. They have an eye, but no head. Stick them into the earring so the eye pokes out at the top.

Salt Dough

Shape the salt dough—tiny fish and birds are easy and fun to do. Before baking, push in an eye pin. After baking, painting, and varnishing your earrings, slip the eye pin over a hook.

Papier-Mâché

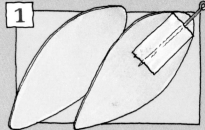

1 Start with two shaped cardboard bases. Tape an eye pin to each base, so that the eye pokes out of the top.

2 Cover with two layers of papier-mâché. Make relief decorations with scrunched-up paper. When dry, cover with latex, paint, and varnish.

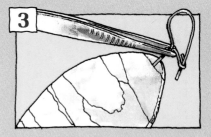

3 Slide the earring pin onto the hook by its eye. Squeeze the hook's wire so the pin won't slip off.

For a really snazzy special effect, rub on sparkling gold paint before varnishing.

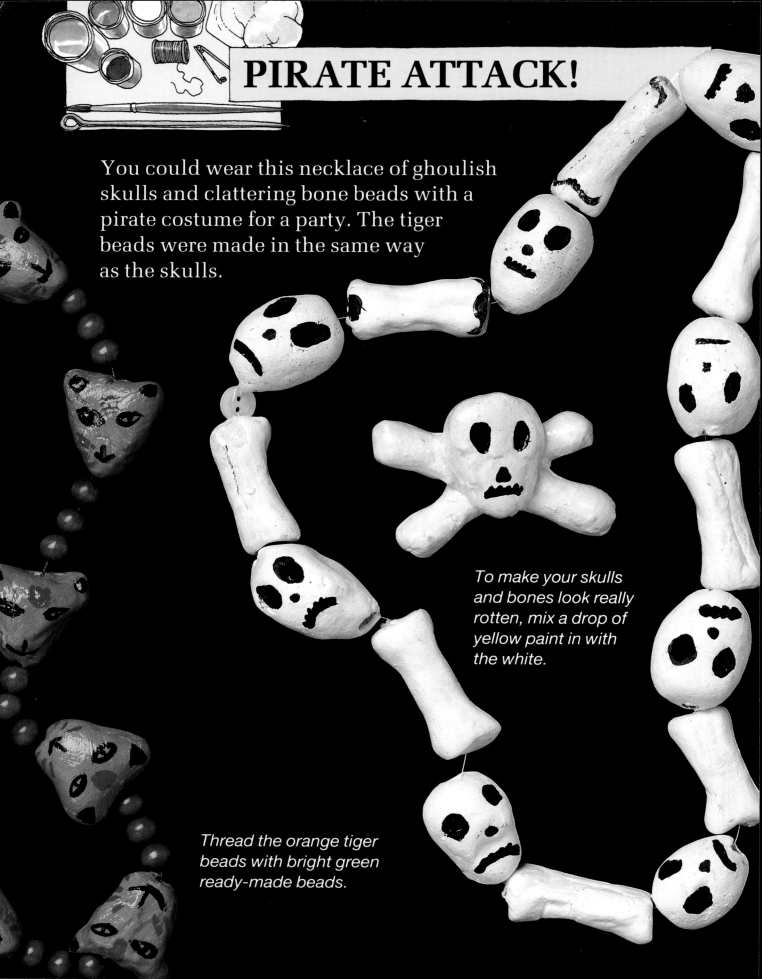

PIRATE ATTACK!

You could wear this necklace of ghoulish skulls and clattering bone beads with a pirate costume for a party. The tiger beads were made in the same way as the skulls.

To make your skulls and bones look really rotten, mix a drop of yellow paint in with the white.

Thread the orange tiger beads with bright green ready-made beads.

1

With your hands, roll some salt dough into a sausage shape about 12 inches long. Cut into eight pieces.

2

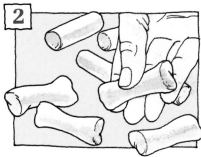

Shape each piece to look like a bone. It's best to pinch the dough in at the middle of the bone and at both ends.

3

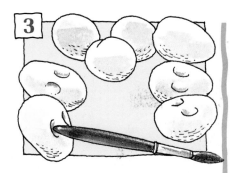

Roll eight balls of salt dough for the skulls. Squeeze in the cheeks. Use the end of a brush to make eye sockets.

4

Push all the beads onto metal skewers and bake in the oven. When cool, give everything a coat of white paint.

5

For extra ghoul-appeal, use black paint to make the skulls' eyes, noses, and mouths really stand out! Then varnish.

6

Thread the skulls and bones. Tie the ends of the thread to a button —it keeps the beads on as you work.

Bony Brooch

Join two bones in the middle with a dab of water, as shown. Press a skull on top.

Smooth the back of the brooch surface. Bake, paint, and varnish, then glue on a finding.

23

SWEET TOOTH

Use colored clay to make this delicious "candy" jewelry. Don't leave your beads lying around though—they look so realistic that someone might end up eating them!

1 Break off small lumps of clay. Roll into balls, then knock each one on your work surface to flatten the edges until you get a cube shape.

2 Make striped "candies" by rolling out layers of different-colored clays. Press them on top of each other, then cut into squares.

3 Roll some clay into a long sausage with your fingers. Wrap a new color around it and press gently. Smooth out where they join.

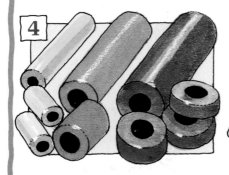

4 Cut the sausage shape into candy-sized beads. Make more in the same way, but change the thickness and cut to different lengths.

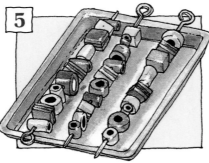

5 Push all your beads onto metal skewers and bake them in the oven, on a baking tray. Follow the instructions on the package carefully.

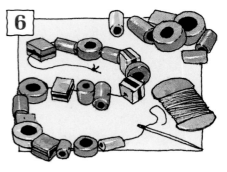

6 When the beads are all cool, thread them onto fine elastic, then knot the ends. You can make a necklace and a matching bracelet.

Make smaller beads for earrings. Use earring findings with head pins (see page 20).

PAPER JEWELRY

Rolled paper beads may look delicate, but the wallpaper paste makes them surprisingly strong. Try using all sorts of colored paper in lots of different thicknesses, as well as newspapers and old magazines.

For earring beads with a large hole, use an eye pin (see page 20), and bend back the pin with tweezers.

1

Make several cardboard templates. Rectangles make simple tube beads. To make oval beads, use a triangle. For fat beads use long templates. For long beads use wide templates.

2

Use the templates to cut out paper triangles and rectangles. To save time, fold the paper in an accordion and draw around the template. Then cut out lots of paper strips at once.

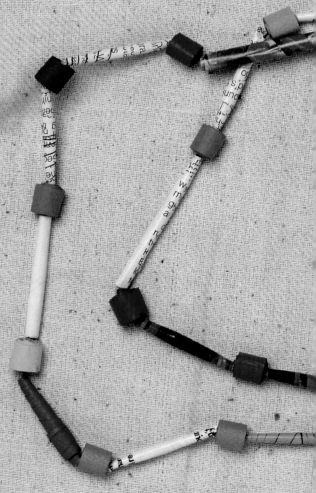

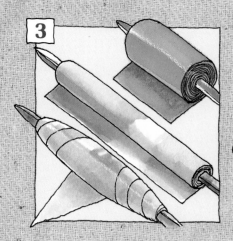

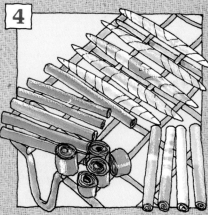

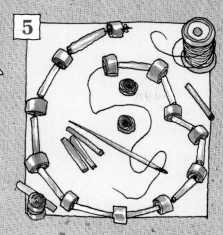

3 Coat both sides of each strip with paste, then roll around a skewer. Roll triangles from their base and rectangles from their short edge.

4 Slide the beads off the skewer and place on a wire rack to give the paste time to dry. There's no need to varnish the beads.

5 Thread the beads through their skewer holes, using strong cotton thread. Finish off by tying the thread with a double knot.

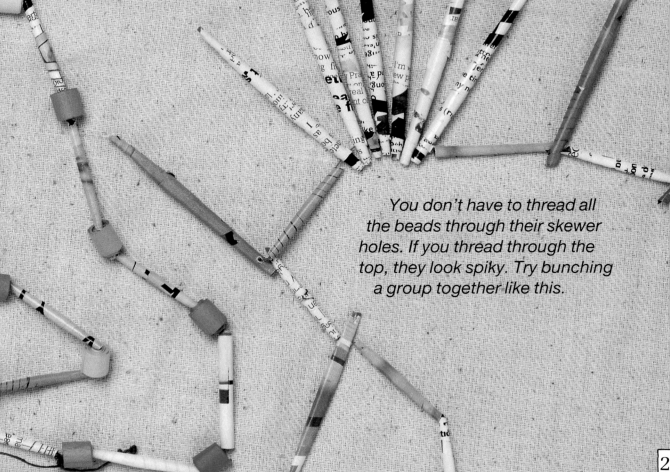

You don't have to thread all the beads through their skewer holes. If you thread through the top, they look spiky. Try bunching a group together like this.

BACK TO NATURE

Natural objects make delicate, unusual necklaces. Collect seeds and leaves outdoors, or raid the kitchen for bay leaves and melon seeds—anything you can find! You'll need to wash melon seeds, place them on paper towels, and leave them to dry in a warm place for a few days. A coat of varnish will give the bay leaves extra strength and shine.

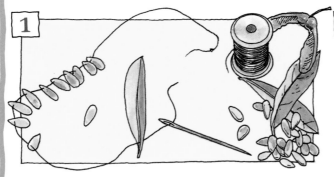

1 Thread a needle. Knot the end of the thread and then push the needle through about ten melon seeds. Then thread a bay leaf.

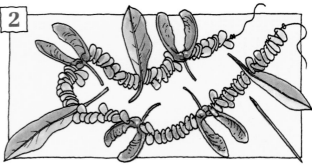

2 Alternate rows of melon seeds and tree seeds or bay leaves. Tie a knot at the end to secure all the seeds and leaves.

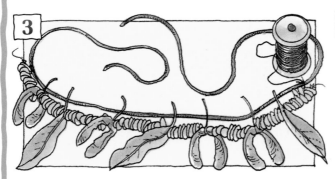

3 Take a length of cord about $2\frac{1}{2}$ feet long. Position the string of seeds in the middle. Now cut another piece of thread and use it to tie one end of the row of seeds to the cord.

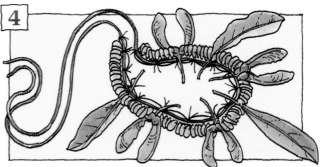

4 Use a double knot to attach the seeds to the cord, about every $\frac{3}{4}$ inch along, until you reach the end. Knot the ends of the cord and your necklace is ready to wear!

Always ask an adult before you gather seeds. Some of them are poisonous.

FELT FRUITS

Squares of felt come in just about every color of the rainbow. Felt is fabulous for making mouthwatering fruits like these.

Felt fruits look great pinned to clothes, bags, or floppy sunhats. Or why not display them in a mini fruit basket?

1

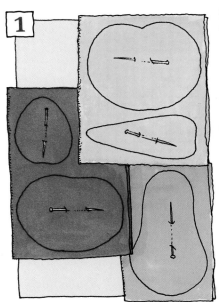

Draw templates for the tangerine, pear, carrot, tomato, and strawberry on paper. Cut them out and pin to scraps of felt.

2

Cut around each template twice. Sew the two halves of each fruit together, leaving a small opening.

3

Stuff each fruit with cotton balls, then sew up the gap. Cut out felt leaves and sew to the top of each fruit.

4

To finish, sew tiny colored beads to the strawberries. Push a tiny safety pin through the back of each fruit.

A Bunch of Cherries

Stitch around a small circle of red felt, then tighten the thread to pull the felt into a ball. Stuff the opening with cotton balls, then finish sewing up the cherry.

Cut thin strips of felt for the stems. Fold in half and stitch down the edge. Sew one to each cherry and pin together in bunches. Add stems to the strawberries, too.

GROOVY GLASSES

Make these swanky glasses for when you feel like some larger-than-life dressing up! Design them in the wackiest shapes you can imagine. Use bold, vivid colors and paint on wild patterns. For the sunburst glasses, build papier-mâché sunrays across the eye holes. Make sure you leave the slits wide enough for you to see through.

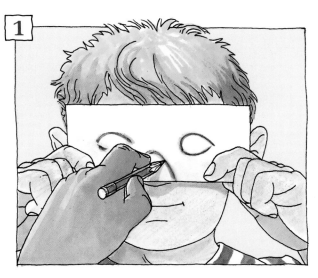

1

Measure across your face and cut a piece of thin cardboard to this width. Hold it to your face and ask a friend to mark where your eyes and nose are.

2

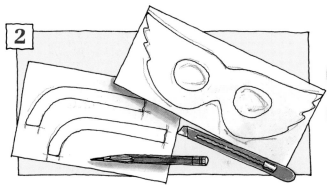

Draw the outline of your glasses and cut them out carefully with a craft knife. Then measure and cut out a pair of arms for your glasses.

3

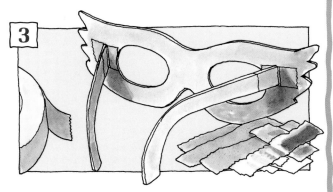

Make a hinge by taping the arms to the glasses with masking tape. Cover with about three layers of papier-mâché. Keep the arm hinges moving as the layers dry so you will be able to fold your finished glasses.

4

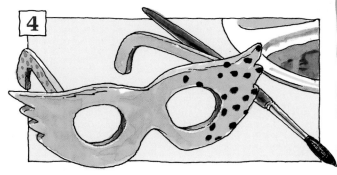

Coat the glasses with white latex, then paint a dazzling pattern in bright acrylic paints. Finish off your groovy glasses with a glossy layer of varnish.

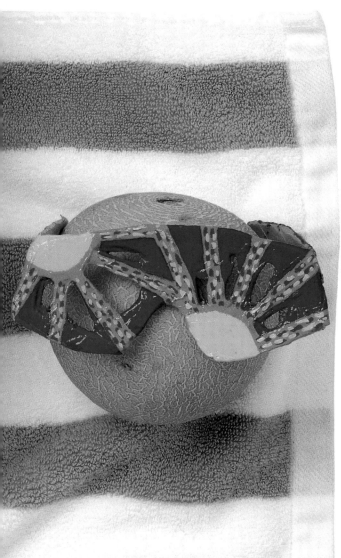

MEGA MEDALS

Ever felt you deserved a medal? Well, now you can wear one that's big enough for everyone to see! The giant pocket watch is papier-mâché, too.

Hang the medals on lengths of ribbon and use gold string for the watch chain.

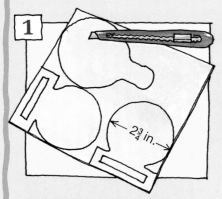

1 Draw the shapes onto thin cardboard and cut them out with a craft knife.

2¾ in.

2 Cover the cardboard bases with two layers of papier-mâché. For a raised watch face, tape on a smaller circle and cover with one more layer.

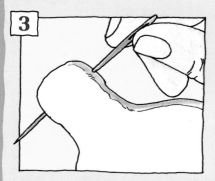

3 Paint and varnish your pieces. Use a darning needle to pierce a hole through the top of the watch for the chain. Reopen the hole after each coat of paint or varnish.

AZTEC JEWELRY

The Aztec people lived in South America hundreds of years ago and their goldsmiths were famous for their dazzling jewelry. Make your own glittering Aztec necklace and a matching ceremonial headdress, encrusted with gems. Finish off with a flourish of bright, colored feathers.

1
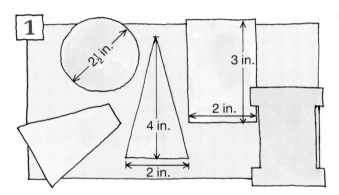

Cut out the cardboard necklace parts —you'll need a circle, two rectangles, and two triangles. Snip the tops of both triangles. Cut into the sides of one of the rectangles, as shown.

2
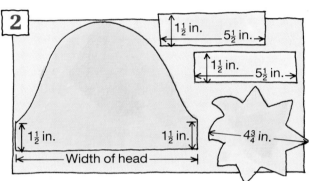

Measure the width of your head, then draw and cut out the headdress front, sides, and star. Bend the headdress so it fits the shape of your head, and then tape on the sides.

3
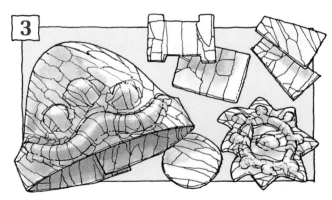

Cover all the shapes with three layers of papier-mâché. Tape scrunched-up paper to the headdress and star for raised decoration (see page 21). Cover with a layer of papier-mâché.

4

Glue spirals of string onto the necklace pieces for relief decoration. Pierce holes with a skewer or a darning needle in the necklace pieces, headdress, and star as shown.

5

Cover the pieces with latex. Then paint the star and necklace pieces a shiny, Aztec gold. Use jade green for the headdress—the Aztecs loved jade.

6

When the headdress is dry, rub gold paint over the green with a cloth. Use a fine brush to paint extra details on all the pieces, then varnish.

7

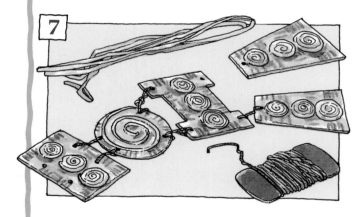

Tie the necklace pieces together with short lengths of sparkling gold string. Use gold raffia at the top to hang the necklace around your neck.

8

Glue brightly colored feathers to the top of your headdress. Use wire to attach the star firmly on top, hiding the glue. Twist the wire at the back.

9

Glue bright felt streamers to the inside of the head-dress, so they flop over the top. To finish, glue on gems, sequins, and coils of string.

SHOWING OFF

Forget about boring old boxes! Why not show the pieces you have made on a crazy jewelry cactus? You can buy scrap wood for the base from a hardware store.

1

Ask an adult to saw a small block of wood (about 7 x 3 x ¾ inch) for a sturdy base.

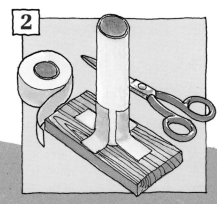

2

Use tape to attach a cardboard tube, such as a toilet-paper roll, to the base.

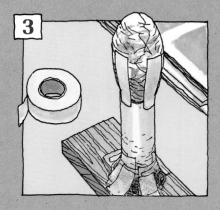

3

Crumple some paper, stuff it into the tube, then tape it in place. This is for attaching your branches.

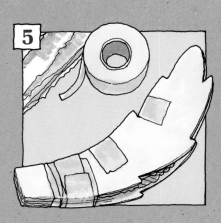

4

Cut out the branches from cardboard. The two large ones have two halves, so cut out four of these.

5

Stuff paper between the two halves of each large branch to pad it out. Hold the sides together with tape.

6

Tape all four branches to the cactus and cover everything with three layers of papier-mâché.

7

Give the cactus a latex base coat and then paint it bright green. Paint on yellow cactus spines, then varnish.

MORE IDEAS

By now you've probably realized that almost anything can be turned into jewelry. Here are a few more ideas you might like to try . . .

Wind some raffia around a cardboard bracelet. Sew embroidery thread in and out of the raffia, adding beads as you go.

Embroidery thread looks great braided. Tie the ends to a barrette, or knot them together to make a friendship bracelet. Add beads if you like.

For a choker, make a salt-dough heart with a hole in the middle. Use pink embroidery thread to sew the heart to a length of velvet ribbon. Glue on two Velcro squares for the fastening, or sew on snaps.

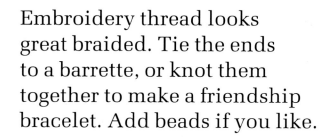

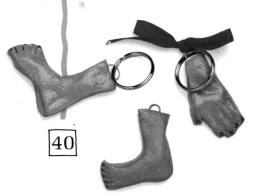

Use salt dough to make these cheerful key chain charms. Push in a paper clip before baking. After painting, slide it onto a key chain— you can buy them from craft stores.